BREAKING OUT OF THE BUNGLE BIRD

Aaron Reynolds

Illustrated by Pete Whitehead

Zonderkidz

Zonderkidz

The children's group of Zondervan

www.zonderkidz.com

Breaking Out of the Bungle Bird
ISBN: 0-310-70956-3

Copyright © 2005 by Willow Creek Association

Requests for information should be addressed to:
Zonderkidz, Grand Rapids, Michigan 49530

Library of Congress Cataloging-in-Publication Data
Reynolds, Aaron, 1970-
  Breaking out of the bungle bird : based on Proverbs 13:10 / written by Aaron Reynolds ; illustrated [by] Peter Whitehead.
    p. cm.
  Summary: Two insects try to escape from the stomach of a bungle bird in this rhyming story based on a Bible verse from the book of Proverbs about the wisdom of taking advice.
ISBN 0-310-70956-3 (hardcover)
 [1. Conduct of life--Fiction. 2. Bible. O.T. Proverbs--Fiction. 3. Insects--Fiction. 4. Escapes--Fiction. 5. Stories in rhyme.] I. Whitehead, Peter, ill. II. Title.
  PZ8.3.R328Br 2005 [E]--dc22

2004012357

Design: Merit Alderink
Art Direction: Michelle Lenger & Merit Alderink

Illustrations used in this book were created digitally using Photoshop.
The body text for this book is set in Triplex Bold and WhoaNelly.

Printed in China
05 06 07 08 09/SCC/5 4 3 2 1

Pride only leads to arguing.
BUT THOSE WHO TAKE ADVICE ARE WISE.
– Proverbs 13:10

In the jungle of Bungle-ma-gungle-ma-tu,
lived a mosquita named Fleeya
and a butterfly, Sue.

Two better best friends
you have never seen—ever.
"And we'll stay bestest friends,"
they would say, "till forever!"

But as sometimes will happen
with friends that are best,
that friendship will sometimes
get put to the test.

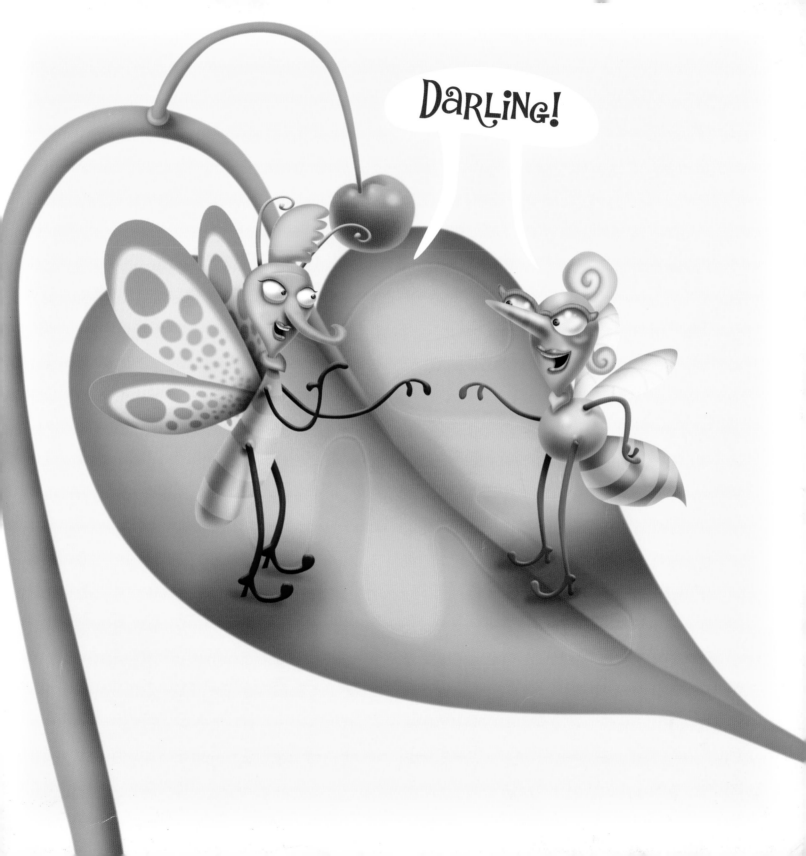

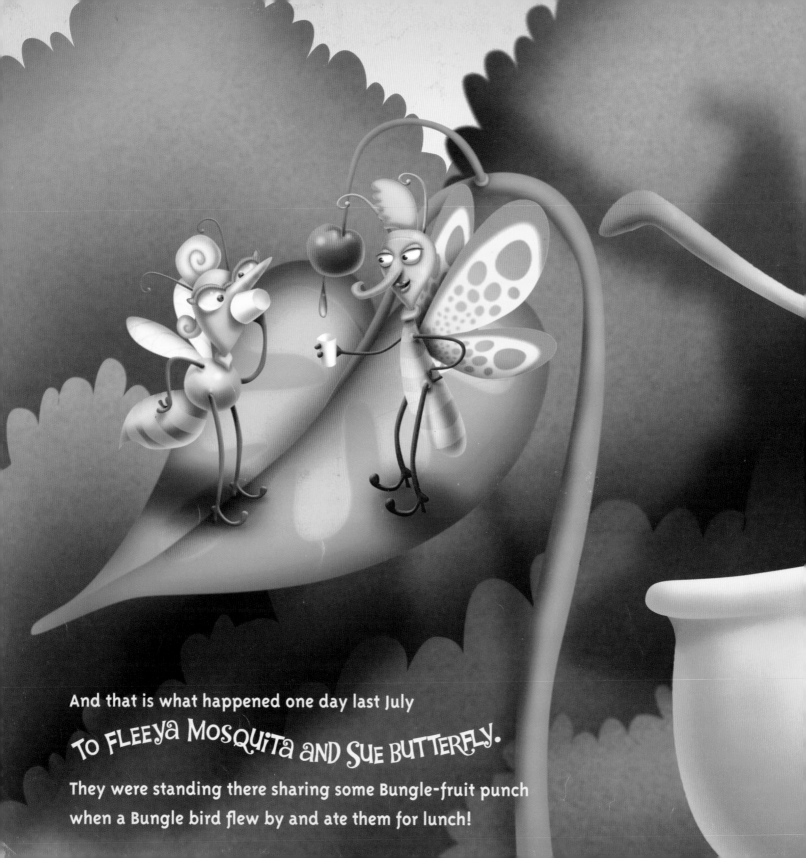

And that is what happened one day last July

To Fleeya Mosquita and Sue Butterfly.

They were standing there sharing some Bungle-fruit punch
when a Bungle bird flew by and ate them for lunch!

and they felt themselves falling.
They tried to crawl up
with their very best crawling.

But they hit with a splash.
The air was quite smelly.
Then they looked.
There they stood
in a Bungle bird belly!

A BUTTERFLY PANIC ATTACK. WAS AT HAND.

If you've ever been eaten, then you understand.
There was only one thought on the mind of Sue now:
We've got to escape from the Bungle Bird. How?

She said, "The time has come for great thoughts to be thinked. For ideas to be hatched. For a plan to be inked."

So silence came over the two in the tummy
of this bird who had thought that these bugs would be yummy.

They thinked, and they thinked, and they think-thinked some more.
They thinked and they thinked till their thinkers were sore.

Until lo and behold, the mosquita named Fleeya
jumped up and said, "Sue! I've got an idea!"

"Oh, BE QUIET, FLEEya," said butterfly Sue.
"You've upset the thinking I'm trying to do!"

Fleeya stood there and tried to pretend
that she hadn't been hurt by her very best friend.

Their problem was tricky—no time to be smug.
After all, digestion waits for no bug.

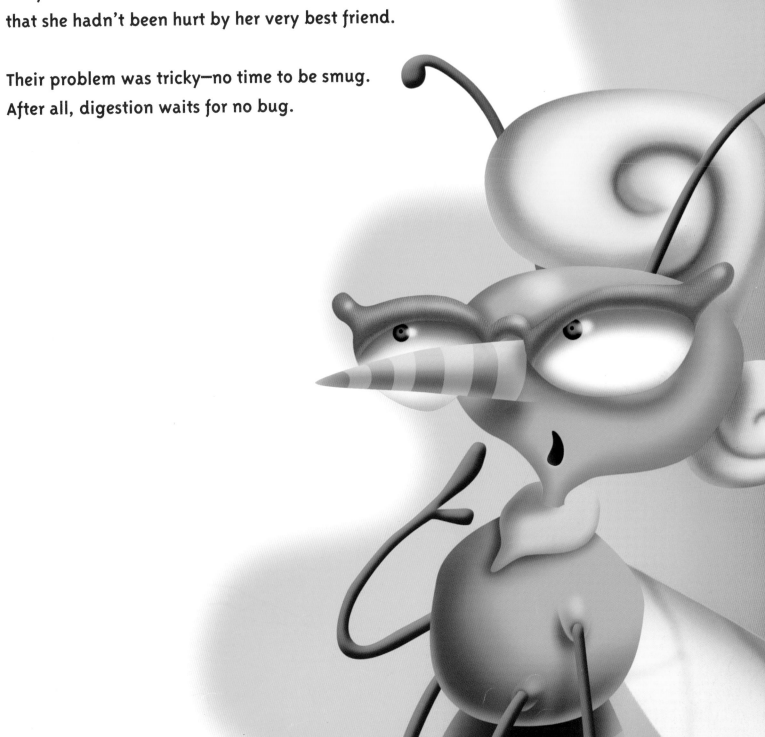

Fleeya tried to be patient. She tried to be true.
And so she just sat there, thinking with Sue.

They thought, and they thought,
and they thought, and they thought,
till their foreheads were wet
and their feelers were hot.

Till Fleeya decided she'd try once again
to spell out her plan TO HER BUTTERFLY FRIEND.

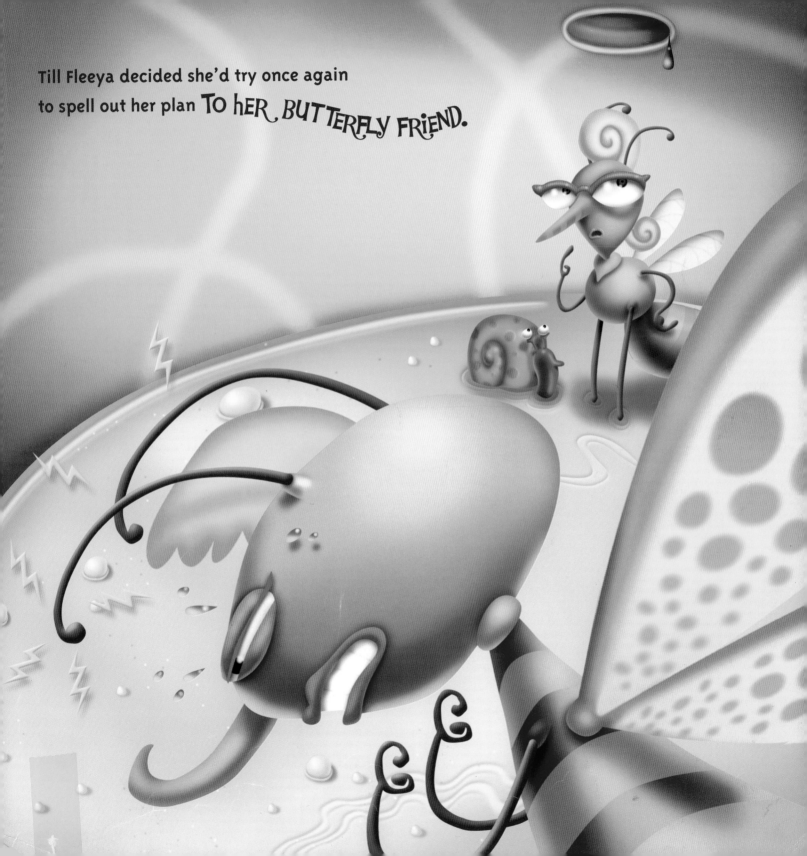

"I'VE GOT IT!" SAID FLEEYA.

"It's not a bad plan."
But Sue stopped her and said,
"You interrupted again!

I'm trying to think of a way to get free,
but I can't concentrate with you yapping at me.
Well, my focus is broken. You might as well tell
of this wonderful plan that you've thought up so well."

And so Fleeya mosquita began to explain
the idea she'd invented inside of her brain.

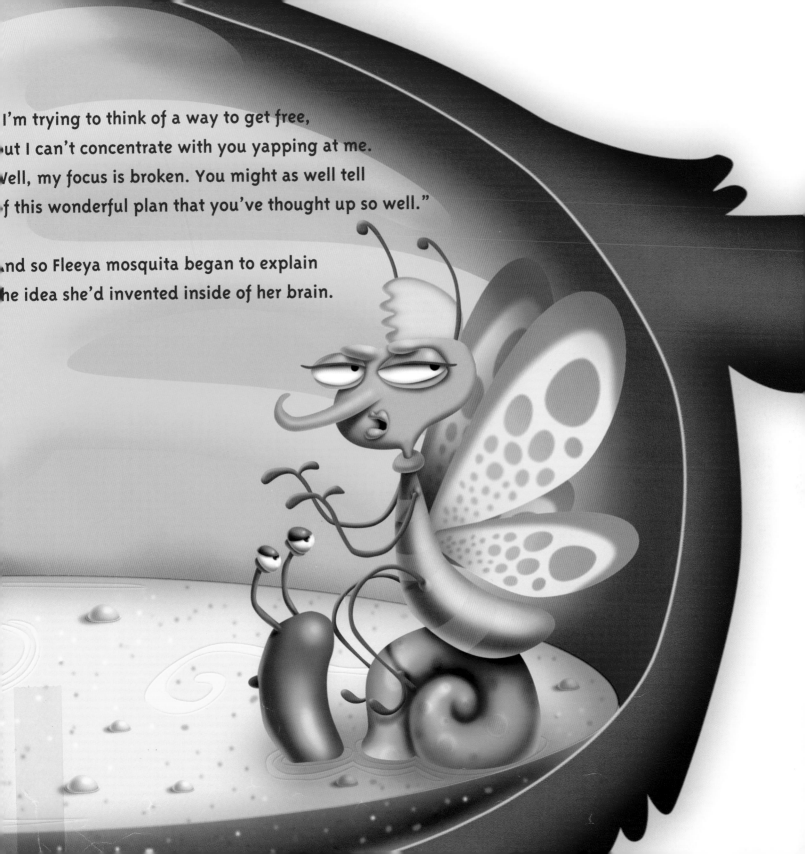

"We could climb up the throat, up high to the head.
Every bird, I think must at last go to bed.

"And when it's asleep—we can tell from the snoring—
we'll pry up its beak and be long gone by morning."

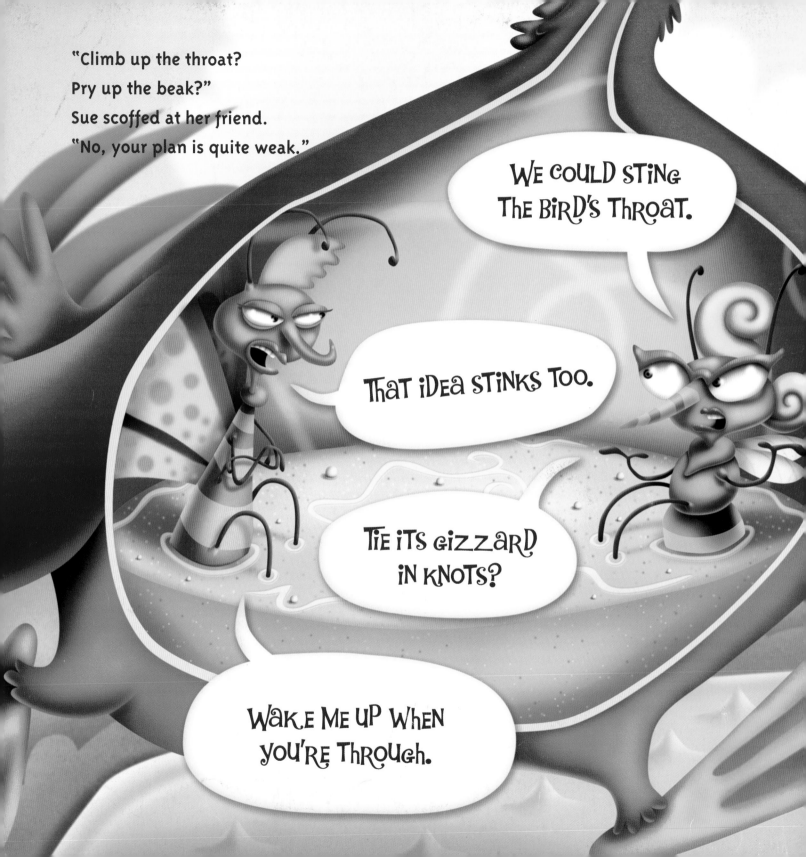

"Climb up the throat?
Pry up the beak?"
Sue scoffed at her friend.
"No, your plan is quite weak."

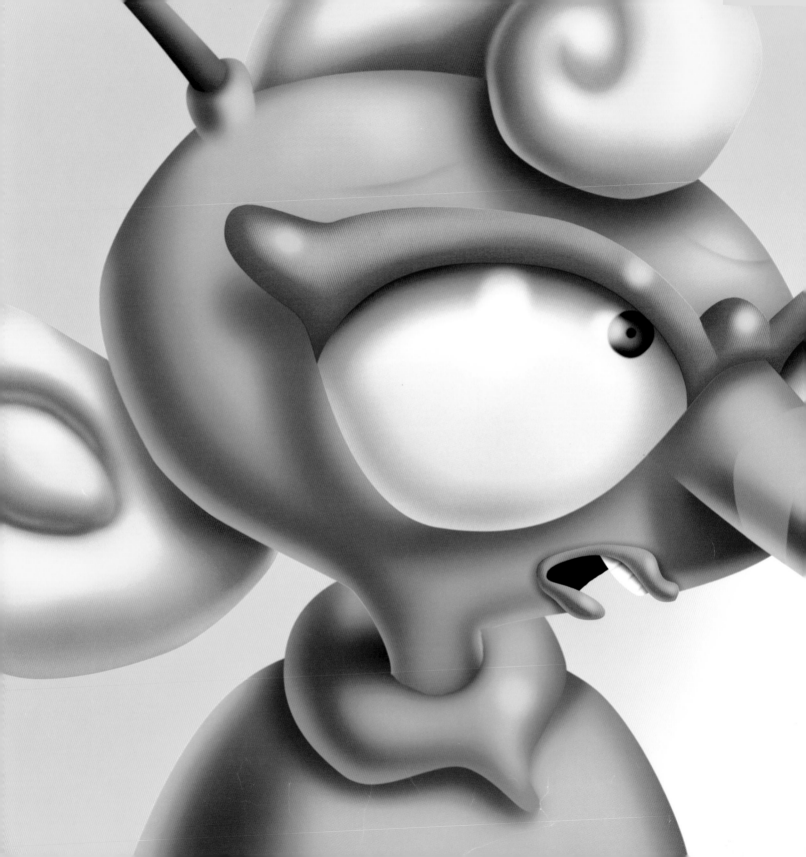

Her list of ideas had come to an end.
Fleeya turned and she looked at her butterfly friend.

"You're my very best friend, but I really can't see—

ALL THESE IDEAS I'VE GOT, YOU WON'T LISTEN TO ME!"

"Yes, Fleeya," Sue said. "You're my friend. This is true.
But that doesn't mean I should listen to you!
I'm older than you. And I'm wise, can't you see?
The one to come up with the plan WILL BE ME."

And so Sue butterfly, she sat down and she thunk.

And she thunk, and she thunk,
and she thunk, and she thunk.
And while she was thunking
and thunking this way,

FLEEya MosquiTa—WELL—She CLiMBeD away.

And later that night, the mosquita got out
up the Bungle bird's throat, through the Bungle bird's mouth.
She slipped out the beak while the bird was asleep,
and she did the whole thing without making a peep.

And, well, not so lucky was butterfly Sue.
SHE NEVER CAME UP WITH THE RIGHT THING TO DO.
The butterfly thought only she knew the way,
so she's probably still in that belly today.

It's really too bad. If she'd taken advice,
then her story, too, might have turned out quite nice.

So, if you ever get eaten and are close to your end,

PLEASE LISTEN AND TAKE THE ADVICE OF YOUR FRIEND.

IT'S a BIRD-EAT-BUG WORLD!

Problems and tough decisions creep and crawl into your life every day. You don't have to figure them all out by yourself. While it may sting to ask a friend for help or admit that you don't have all the answers, the truth is, there are lots of wise people fluttering around in your life just buzzing with great advice.

METAMORPHOSIS CHALLENGE

Put your feelers to work and figure out one or two friends that you could ask for advice if you needed it. When you face a pesky decision or problem, go and ask their advice. And if they offer it without you asking, listen! Just because someone offers you advice doesn't mean you should always do it. Buzz over to the Bible and see if the advice matches what God has to say about your problem.

According to Proverbs 13:10, wise people don't act like they know it all. They take good advice! Of course, you could just ignore good advice when you hear it and wind up like Sue. On the other hand, maybe it's best not to think about what happened to Sue.